HELLO
OCEAN

Pam Muñoz Ryan ❋ Illustrated by Mark Astrella

SCHOLASTIC INC.

New York Toronto London Auckland Sydney
Mexico City New Delhi Hong Kong Buenos Aires

Hello, ocean,
my old best friend.

I'm here,
with the five of me, again!

I see the ocean,
gray, green, blue,
a chameleon
always changing hue.

Amber seaweed,
speckled sand,

bubbly waves
that kiss the land,

wide open water
before my eyes,

reflected in a
bowl of skies,

glistening tide pools
and secret nooks—
I love the way
the ocean **looks**.

I **hear** the ocean,
a lion's roar,
crashing rumors
toward the shore,

water
shushing
and
rushing
in,

then
whispering
back to
the sea
again.

Froggy songs from distant boats,
gentle clangs from bobbing floats,

screak of gulls
calling down—

I love the way
the ocean **sounds**.

I **touch** the ocean,
and the surf gives chase,
then wraps me in a wet embrace.

Pulling,
pushing,
the restless sea
repeats the same
refrain to me.

Waves that pounce
in rowdy play,

tide that tickles
with splashing spray,

squishy,
sandy,
soggy ground,

slippery seaweed that wraps around,

sudden breezes
that make me squeal—
I love the way
the ocean **feels**.

I **smell** the ocean,
the fresh salt wind,
wafting lotions
from suntanned skin.

Aromas from some ancient tale
disclose their news when I inhale.

Reeky fish from waters deep,

fragrant ore from holes dug steep,

drying kelp
and musty shells—
I love the way
the ocean **smells**.

I **taste** the ocean
and wonder why
it tastes like tears
I sometimes cry.

Sandy grains in a salty drink

are best for fish and whales, I think.

I lick the drops
still on my face;
I love the way
the ocean **tastes**.

The sun dips down;
it's time to go.
But I'll be back
to see your show,

hear the stories you have to spin,
taste your flavors once again,

take deep sniffs
of briny air,
and feel the treasures
you have to share.

Goodbye, ocean,
my old best friend. . . .

ISBN 0-439-40317-0

Text copyright © 2001 by Pam Muñoz Ryan. Illustrations copyright © 2001 by Mark Astrella. All rights reserved. Published by Scholastic Inc., 557 Broadway, New York, NY 10012, by arrangement with Charlesbridge Publishing. SCHOLASTIC and associated logos are trademarks and/or registered trademarks of Scholastic Inc.

12 11 10   13 14/0

Printed in the U.S.A.   08

First Scholastic printing, January 2002

Illustrations done in acrylics on airbrush paper
Display type and text type set in Goudy Oldstyle and Leawood
Designed by Paige Davis